T0146595

TURKON,
A STRIPLING
YOUNG WARRIOR

Turkon and Richelle

STERLING DAY

BALBOA.
PRESS
A DIVISION OF HAY HOUSE

Balboa Press books may be ordered through booksellers or by contacting:

Balboa Press
A Division of Hay House
1663 Liberty Drive
Bloomington, IN 47403
www.balboapress.com
1 (877) 407-4847

Print information available on the last page.

ISBN: 978-1-5043-6865-0 (sc)
ISBN: 978-1-5043-6866-7 (e)

Balboa Press rev. date: 11/28/2016

TABLE OF CONTENTS

INTRODUCTION

This book is paraphrased and fictionalized from the story of the "2,000 stripling young warriors," from the Book of Mormon and in the book of Alma, Chapters 56 - 59. The Book of Mormon is considered by it's adherents as holy scripture, just as much as the Bible. This sacred book is considered to be another testament of Christ, because within these pages, the Savior appeared to the inhabitants of America after His resurrection.

Just as one could take the story of David & Goliath, and imagine what David's life was like growing up in ancient Israel, so I did with the fictional life of Turkon, although I stayed on script with what actually happened within the Book of Mormon.

I hope my readers enjoy what it would be like to be a part of this grand undertaking.

CHAPTER 1

THE DEPARTURE

The Nephites (Nee-fights) had fair skin, whereas their enemies, the Lamanites (lay-mun-nights) were quite dark, just as their descendants, the Native Americans. The Nephites wore clothes and were herdsmen and farmers, whereas the Lamanites wore a loin cloth and were hunters and warlike. The Nephites belonged to the Church of Christ, and missionaries were sent to convert the Lamanites. Surprisingly, a large group of Lamanites were converted by the Nephite, Ammon, which caused the majority of Lamanites to anger. They threatened to kill this group unless they rescinded their new religion. The year of our Lord was now the 26th year of the reign of judges.

Refusing to deny the Savior, they were willing to die for their new cause. They threw down their swords and vowed to never murder again. Then they bowed before the onslaught and the Lamanites began mowing them down like sheep. The scene became so bloody that many of the Lamanites were sickened and refused to kill any more of these strange people. In fact, the entire Lamanite army stopped the slaughter and allowed these zealots to go.

The Nephites had heard about this group of converted Lamanites and gave them a large part of their lands to raise their herds and children and vowed to protect them from further abuse. They became known as the people of Ammon, because the Nephite missionary Ammon had converted them through the Spirit of the Lord.

Besides hunting wild animals, the Lamanites liked to raid the Nephites for property and possessions, after killing the inhabitants. Their hatred of the Nephites was passed down from father to son for hundreds of generations. In fact, the Lamanites had already attacked and brought down many fortified Nephite cities, as they vastly outnumbered the Nephites. The situation had become desperate for the Nephite army, and General Moroni (Ma-roh-n(long i) asked his trusted friend, Captain Helaman (Heel-a-mun), to go to the People of Ammon, and see if he could rustle up some much needed support. "I'll do my best," vowed Helaman. Arriving there, he sent out a petition asking for help. Helaman was a very large man in stature as well in spirit and in body. Standing six foot four with broad shoulders and a muscular physique, weighing about 245, he looked ominous in any situation, but especially in armor. He looked particularly menacing. He had a plume atop his helmet, and it added a dash of flare about him. He walked with an air of royalty, but in reality, he was down to earth and as friendly to the lowliest soldier as he was with those above him. He walked with the confidence of a hero, which in fact, he was.

The men in his charge were extremely loyal to him, and in fact, most of the men he led in the past would risk their life for him, which was sometimes necessary. But in this leadership role, he and his young warriors were literally with their backs against a wall. The ubiquitous Lamanites seemed like a never-ending stream of killing machines. For every savage you killed, it seemed there were two more to take his place. In reality, they were outnumbered approximately two to one.

The Lamanites wore nothing but a breech cloth and moccasins to cover their nakedness, and they painted their bodies with blood or red paint to appear more ferocious. To ameliorate their chances against the onslaught, the Nephites realized they needed to wear strong armor to give them a better chance of winning. The Nephites obviated any trouble, whereas the Lamanites were the attackers in order to gain the Nephite's wealth and lands. The Nephites were fighting for their lives, and the lives of their wives and children; their flocks and their religion.

The town's elders arrived and helplessly explained that they had covenanted with God to never raise their swords again, and buried their weapons of war, and vowed to God to never shed blood again. But feeling guilty they're not doing their fair share in the war, they were willing to break their oath to help their benefactors, the Nephites.

Helaman was dumb struck. "No! Absolutely not!" he replied with gravitas. Helaman knew the seriousness of making the covenant with God, and if they were to break this oath, he feared they could lose their souls. Besides, they desperately needed Providence's help at this time. In the meantime, a petition was sent throughout the people of Ammon, and was brought back with the signatures of 2,000 young warriors, ages 14 to 19.

The most respected High Priest, Samuel, read it aloud. "We,

the sons of those who covenanted to never shed blood again, but so were not there when the oath was given, wish to submit our humble request to fight with you for our liberties, our fathers and our mothers; and support the Nephite armies in any way that we can.

We are not afraid, nor fear death, for our mothers have taught us from our youth to have faith in God. And should we die, we can stand before Christ with a pure conscience." When Helaman heard this, the venerable captain was so impressed that he silently wept with joy to hear such great courage from so young of heart.

Helaman rode on a beautiful white stallion, and he looked very strong and noble while riding it. The young warriors quickly gathered their needed supplies and food and placed them into the numerous supply wagons, kissed their mothers, hugged their fathers and siblings with many tears, and got ready to march confidently behind their leader. They were so striking in spirit and in body that Helaman referred to them as his "stripling young warriors." In fact, from then on, he referred to them as "his sons," and loved them as much as his own. Helaman was truly a man to match the mountains.

But before he joined his unit, Turkon made sure he also gave a passionate hug to his youthful sweetheart, Richelle, who was also seventeen. With dark flowing silky straight hair down to her waist, and large, dark eyes set in a sculpted face, he knew he was a lucky kid to have this soul-mate. She had a delicate, small nose, and smooth lips to guard her dainty mouth.

Picture of Richelle

Turkon looked at her as one would worship a goddess. Her mother married a Nephite, so she looked like she had a permanent tan. Turkon was much darker, owing to his Lamanite ancestry. "Whatever happens," she said, "I will be faithful to you, and you can count on me to be here when you return." You can imagine Turkon's joy when he heard those words. And with the knowledge that there was no one left his age to entice her also calmed his mind.

Many of Turkon's friends were envious of his catch, and expressed it openly. Turkon knew he was blessed by having her love. He comforted her and dried her tears as best he could, holding back his own youthful sobs, assuring her that it was God's will, and to know that if he survived this war, he would come back for her. Her warm breath on his made him ache for her, but he knew that any kissing would just inflame their passions more.

"Why must you go?" she begged. Why can't God bless our love and let us live in peace? But I know I sin in my desire, for it must be that we help our nation defeat the blood-thirsty Lamanites. Be careful my love, and may God be with you." "I will, Richelle. I don't intend to let you or my people down. I want to be a valiant warrior in a righteous cause." Her warm breath on his inflamed his passions, and so he broke away from her. He knew that pure virtue was more priceless than diamonds in the Lord's eye, and he wasn't about to lose it in the least degree.

And with that, he joined his infantry unit. He took his place in front of the unit, which was called a company, because he was the oldest member of the 100 warriors he was placed in command. Most of the boys in his company were 15 or 16; not old enough to shave.

With the 2,000 stripling young soldiers, Helaman divided them into two battalions, with ten companies in each battalion. After everything was duly organized, they marched off to their destiny. Richelle and others watched them march into and over the horizon, with flags flying. Oh, how proud Turkon was to be a part of this great adventure. He struggled to keep the butterflies in his stomach at bay.

Illustrated by S. Day

Turkon holding sword

Turkon was to lead the fourth company in the second battalion. It was Turkon's duty to take care of any of the situations or problems for the 100 boys under his command, so as to not bother Helaman with any petty problems. Of course, any serious problem would necessitate bringing it under the attention of the Captain. The four guard dogs were allowed to roam at their leisure, but they were loyal enough to eventually return from time to time.

The young men would march under Turkon 10 abreast and 10 deep, forming a perfect square of 100 individuals, along with the other nine companions in his battalion. Turkon stationed himself in the upper right hand corner of his company, where he could be seen by his warriors. The young men were not required to march in-step, but were admonished to stay within their chosen space. For example, number four, six would be in the fourth row back and the sixth man within that row.

The march ended up being a six day adventure, and many of the boys developed blisters, as they were not used to marching. Other complaints Turkon received were stomach ailments, fevers, and home sickness, although most of the boys kept their home sicknesses to themselves, so as to not admit their youthful inexperience. Other problems which caused individuals to temporarily leave the formation were to remove thorns from their feet which had penetrated through their moccasins, bee stings wherein Turkon removed the stingers, and heat exhaustion, where the sufferer needed to be bathed in cool water to bring down his temperature.

Other problems were poisonous vipers in the way of the first company, which caused the leader of that battalion to stop while they removed the reptile and place them from harm's way. (Of course, all the companies behind the first had to stop also). All that marching caused the young men to be ravenously hungry. Because their parents made sure their sons would eat well the first few days before the fruit got rotten and the bread moldy, they placed the food in the 30 wagons that Helaman and his wagon drivers had brought with them. Helaman slept in the tent with his wagon masters.

Bread, carrots, potatoes, beef, chicken, bacon and more had been generously donated. Turkon's dad even submitted a large chunk of honeycomb for his son to enjoy. Ten thousand pounds of beef jerky was also rounded up. The young men enjoyed some fruit for breakfast, and five four ounce pieces of jerky each to chew on while marching until dusk, as they didn't stop for lunch. At dusk, they set up camp with the tents, which held 20 men each.

Fires were made throughout the camp by striking obsidian against their steel knives which each boy carried by his side. Sparks would land in the tinder, and by blowing on an ember, fire was produced, which got going nicely by adding more wood. In this way, they could warm themselves and cook the meat, as well as keeping the insects and predators at bay. By boiling the water in large kettles, they killed any parasites or bacteria which might be in the local water supply.

Helaman rode his white stallion in front of the two battalions he had recruited, and the 30 wagons brought to carry their supplies contained many blankets and tents, as well as their food supply. The wagons followed from behind so as to not heed their progress. Since the tents held 20 men each, Turkon received a total of five tents for his company. Each company required a guard to watch through the night for about four hours, and then another person was required to take his place so everyone could receive some shut eye.

Tents at sunset with young warriors

Turkon volunteered to do the first guard, so as to set a good example. Others were chosen by the numbers, one to fifty with one going first. One night the guard woke up Turkon from the warm blanket he was cuddled under to be told that he heard one of the boys sniffling. Turkon followed the sniffling sounds to the northwest corner of the tent, where 14 year old Benjamin was laying.

Turkon put his arm around the young lad and making as little noise as possible so as to not wake anyone up, he asked in a whisper what was wrong.. "I'm sorry I woke you up, Turkon. I can't help it. I miss my family, especially my mother." "Well, don't worry about it. I reckon we're all missing our families by now. We're just trying really hard to keep it to ourselves. You'll be alright. Just close your eyes and think good thoughts." And with that, Turkon covered him with his wool blanket, and cradled Ben's head to his chest and slowly rocked him until he was out.

Turkon thought the worst part of surviving the march as well as sleeping were the ubiquitous insects which swarmed him and his men continually. There were mosquitos that enjoyed feasting on his blood, which was good for the "skeeters," but not so good for the boys. And then the gnats and flies would relish flying into their eyes and nostrils at breakneck speeds.. Some of the men resorted to covering their bare skin with mud to prevent the bites and their accompanying incessant pain and itching.

Of course their 320 mile march necessitated crossing streams and a couple of large rivers that were about 30 feet across, but the currents were slow enough to enable the warriors to swim across without too much difficulty. Turkon enjoyed the rivers because Helaman allowed the young men to bathe in the cool waters and feel refreshed for a few minutes before Helaman requested them to hurry.

"Faster, faster, he would cajole his young men to speed their march up from time to time. It was imperative that they reach their destination as quickly as possible.

There was one time they stopped under a 235 foot waterfall

with the accompanying mists spraying those who were close to it. It seemed everyone took turns enjoying the cool mists, dancing their magic like a thousand tiny fairies over their tired, perspiring bodies. So far, things were going as smoothly as could be expected under trying circumstances. And again, Helaman allowed a small respite from the incessant marching. A few of the men who were out of shape or carrying extra body weight were allowed to sit for a while in the wagons to catch their breath, as each wagon was pulled by two horses. But they were expected to return to their proper units as soon as they could. One kid had a high fever, so he rode in a wagon for three days before his elevated temperature subsided.

One of the young men in Turkon's company was a boy the others called chubby, because he weighed 223 pounds while standing 5'10. Chubby was a name they used in endearment, because he seemed to be able to bring a smile to the grumpiest kid. He was just the kind of person that you liked to have around to lighten your stress. But all that marching caught up to him, so Turkon allowed him to ride in the wagon whenever he needed to.

Helaman told his young warriors they were headed to the large, fortified city of Judea. Many of the Nephite cities sounded Hebrew, because hundreds of years earlier the Nephites and Lamanites, who shared the same father (Lehi), had originally come from Jerusalem in a large boat. The Lord warned Lehi in a very vivid dream or "vision," to take his family and leave Jerusalem, along with the "daughters of Ishmael," as the city was about to be destroyed by its enemies. Nephi (knee-figh), the younger brother, believed his father, and those who followed him became the Nephites. They were a God-fearing people, and Nephi became their leader.

When they landed in "the land of promise," (America), the Lamanites, who were named after Nephi's older brother, Laman (Lay-man), and his younger brother, Lemuel, rebelled against their father, condemning him by saying they left their comfortable home (Lehi was a very rich merchant) to chase his dreams. They took a large contingent of men and women with them into the "wilderness." They were culpable of being blood thirsty people, living by hunting wild animals and plundering the Nephites whenever and wherever they could.

The Nephites raised wheat, barley, vegetables, fruit trees, and herded cattle, sheep, pigs, and a few horses. They were usually a peace-loving people, who worshipped God and thanked Him for His help. So when the two groups fought, the Lamanites fought for plunder, along with their deep hatred for the Nephites. On the other hand, the Nephites, who were vastly outnumbered two to one, fought for their wives, children, animal herds, and their religion. A big difference in their motivations.

They were averaging anywhere from 40 to 50 miles a day before they set up camp, made fires, and fed the horses. Helaman knew they were about a day's march from Judea, so he warned his boys to be prepared for battle anytime, in case the Lamanite spies found them marching towards the city. The young men became more apprehensive, and said more fervent prayers that night.

The next morning, they spent less time at breakfast than

usual, and got a head start towards Judea. They marched double time in order to get to Judea before dusk, but were surprised to see no Lamanites. Helaman had told them that the Lamanites had surrounded the city. What happened? Turns out the Lamanite scouts had observed Helaman's army, and had run to the Lamanite king, Ammoron, to inform him of the Nephite reinforcements. Ammoron then immediately sent a message to the Lamanites surrounding the city to retreat. Evidently, they thought Helaman's 2,000 warriors represented a much larger army.

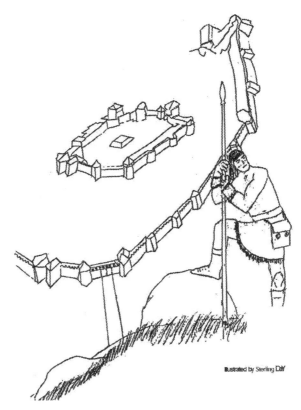

Illustrated by Sterling Day

Son of Heleman rest near Antiparah

CHAPTER 2

PREPARING FOR BATTLE

The city of Judea was situated about 420 miles southeast of the capital Zarahelma, where the Nephites would march their prisoners to, and between the Nephite cities of Antiparah and Nephihah. The soldiers were toiling mightily during the process of making fortifications for the city. Great heaps of soil were built up around Judea by digging deep ditches and placing the dirt to make a wall where timbers could be placed on top of the mounds. These timbers were approximately six feet high. Towers were constructed every 200 yards for the guards to observe enemy movements.

The city encompassed around 20,000 citizens, with another 10,000 soldiers and their wives and children being allowed to be with their husbands and fathers. This brought the total population within the city walls to approximately 60,000 inhabitants. The Nephite soldiers were tired and depressed, both in body and spirit, as they continued building fortifications around the city after losing many battles. Already, the cities of Zeezrom, Cumeni, and Antiparah had fallen into enemy hands. This defensive wall was about four miles long and 6 miles across. Receiving supplies was a constant problem, but thanks to a clear stream running through the center of town, water was plentiful.

Captain Antipus was assigned to lead the Nephites. He was admonished to protect the city at all costs. The Lamanites had already overrun many of the Nephite strongholds, and General Moroni instructed Antipus to fight to the death, if need be, and never surrender. Antipus was delighted to see "Helaman's sons," shore up his weakened army. Captain Antipus was not nearly as physically strong as Helaman, but he was just as strong spiritually. He had a good, tactical mind for warfare, and he was as brave and stalwart as any officer, if not better.

He stood 6'2" in height and weighed about 195. With his blonde hair and deep set blue eyes, he was as handsome a figure as anyone. After hearing Helaman's explanation for his 2,000 stripling young warriors, he wiped a silent tear or two after seeing that these stripling young warriors were more than willing to help their Nephite benefactors fight their battles. "What courage! What honor!" he thought. And they were quick to follow instructions, and as far as Turkon knew, nobody was murmuring about their circumstances either.

Antipus' army had fought many skirmishes with the Lamanites already, and were chased from city to city until they were instructed to make their last stand in the heavily fortified city of Judea. One major factor which helped the Nephites was their armor. They had breast, leg, arm, and head armor to protect their bodies from the slings of arrows, spears, axes, and knives and swords. But the bare skin of the Lamanite were easily punctured and sliced against the Nephite weapons.

Still, the Lamanites proved to be an impressive foe. Bloodthirsty and barbaric, they were determined to wipe the Nephites off the face of the earth. Their chiseled bodies showed their way of life, which was cruel and uncompromising. As a general rule, the Lamanites were in better shape than the Nephites, but there were also many exceptions. For example, the Nephite officers were in superior shape. But most of their soldiers planted crops and herded animals for a living, whereas the Lamanites were taught to hunt as soon as they could carry a weapon.

Heaven help you if you were taken prisoner, because you became a sordid display of sadistic torture, in which even the women and children were encouraged to join the festivities before they were mercifully killed. The only Nephites they kept prisoner were the officers. The Lamanite children were encouraged to torture the insects and other small game for sport before killing them.

The Lamanites painted their entire bodies red, shaved off all their hair, and wore only a loin cloth around their privates, with moccasins on their feet. After each battle, the Nephites dug deep pits to throw the dead bodies in, both Lamanite and Nephite. They kept the Nephite armor and weapons to use for another day. They told Helaman and his sons to go through the armor and weapons and choose the ones they wanted, as there were more than enough.

Rather than watching his young army have a free-for-all, Helaman instructed the company leaders to send them in one at a time to avoid bedlam. After the first three companies had their pick, it was time for Turkon's men to go through the pile. Turkon was able to pick one of the finer swords, and armor that didn't have too many dents and punctures.

Each young man was required to clean the blood off of their own equipment. Both Lamanite and Nephite blood was found in different quantities on every item. The Nephite soldiers told Helaman's young men that in a heated battle, blood would spray everywhere, including in your eyes, making it difficult to see. It would also be difficult to hang onto your swords, as they would become slippery with the warm liquid. That was why each sword had a cross-guard to protect their hands from slipping onto the sharp blades.

Antipus was pleased to see his men take the sons of Helaman under their wing and explain to them the art of warfare. They were patient in their instructions, and resisted the urge to yell at them. The stripling young warriors picked things up fast, and became good sword fighters in their own right.

The fact that the soldiers now had plenty of time to prepare for battle had plenty of time to rest from previous battles was a real blessing. Helaman and Antipus would drill the men daily; exercises to build up muscles and stamina. Daily marches outside the gates, where Helaman's young men learned how to march in step. Simulated sword fights using wooden, unsharpened swords to train them in the proper way to use them. Excursions into the woods to find game added to their dwindling food supply.

To pass the time of day during his idle time, Turkon befriended one of the town's boys named Teancum. Teancum was approximately Turkon's age, and they would play soccer with the other boys had a ball. Turkon could play with the best of them. Also, Teancum's cat had a litter of kittens, and he gave the white one to Turkon. This kitten gave Turkon hours of pleasure as he teased the kitten with twine, and the cat would snuggle up to Turkon's warm body when it was time to sleep. He named his cat Whiskers, and he now was a year old and almost fully grown.

Also, Turkon still had the responsibility of taking care of the boys in his company as best he could. Turkon was pleased to see that Chubby was now a lean, muscled warrior, no longer the pudgy kid. Everyone in his company was in better shape than they had ever been before, and they were itching for a fight. Their wish would soon come to pass before anyone's prediction.

Helaman's small army arrived in town during the 26th year of the judges. It was now the 27th year of the judges. Imagine everybody's surprise and joy when the 2,000 warrior's fathers sent large amounts of food and clothing to the hungry inhabitants. Turkon especially was thankful for the fine winter coat his father sent him, as it had a fur lining made out of foxes, as winter was beginning to set in. Fresh fruit and vegetables; including melons, squash, pumpkins, corn, potatoes apples, pears, venison, chicken, beef, fish, and pork. Not to mention the hundreds of bushels of wheat to make breads with. Enough food to keep everyone fed for weeks.

Another pleasant surprise were letters from home. But the letter Turkon was most excited to read was the one from Richelle. It read:

Dear Turkon,

Words cannot express my continued love for you. Everyone in the land miss their sons. The older men now have more work to do, picking fruit and herding animals, so us girls are helping their fathers more. But we really don't mind, as it is for a good cause. Every night when I kneel next to my bed, I thank my Heavenly Father for all my blessings, and beg him to keep you safe and to bring you home for me someday. It's been more than a year now since I saw you last, and my love is continually burning within my heart. In fact, if anything, it burns brighter than ever. I think it's a miracle that you haven't had to fight yet.

I am not as strong as your mother, but I am trying real hard to be like her. Sometimes I find myself being weak, crying myself to sleep at night. I visit with your parents every day, and your mother and I reminisce about the good times we shared with you. Your Dad likes to tease me about our youthful love, but I'm sure it's his way of coping with the situation. I enjoyed helping your Mom bake cakes and loaves of bread for you. Please write back to me and tell me how you are doing.

With all my love,
Richelle

Wow, with a letter like that, how can you not rejoice for such sweet loved ones. He also was thankful for all of his blessings, and knew that God was in charge of <u>all things.</u> He prayed daily for deliverance from their enemies. Only time would tell whether that was meant to be or not.

At this time, another 2,000 Nephite soldiers joined Antipus' army from Zarahemla, increasing his army to 12,000. Because the armies of Helaman and Antipus now numbered 14,000, they felt strong enough to take on the Lamanite army. But Ammoron was afraid to take on the Nephites head-on, telling his armies to continue hiding behind the city walls of Zeezrom, Cumeni, and Antiparah.

CHAPTER 3

THE BATTLE

The Nephites sent out spies to make sure the Lamanites didn't try to sneak past Judah in an effort to conquer other cities, as the other Nephite cities were not sufficiently strong enough to resist their attacks. In the meantime, the Lamanites were beginning to be increasingly anxious seeing all the supplies and reinforcements the city of Juda was receiving. Antipus and Helaman put their heads together and formulated a stratagem to trap the Lamanite army.

They decided to send Helaman's small army of boys towards a neighboring city as if they were carrying supplies to them. Then if the Lamanite army pursued them, Antipus would march his army towards the Lamanites from the rear, thus taking them by surprise. After rounding up his army, and having them put on their armor and gathering up their swords, Helaman explained to his "sons,", as they were worthy to be called his sons, their stratagem. Every one of them cheered as they realized they were finally going to see some action. Then they all knelt as Helaman asked for providential help in this endeavor.

Turkon could hardly contain the butterflies in his stomach as he marched his 100 men, along with the others, outside the city gates. The hairs along the back of his neck stood up in anticipation of a possible battle. They marched double-time northward, and when they retired that night, their spies informed them that the largest of all the Lamanite armies was pursuing them.

After marching double time almost continually, except for short bursts of rest, and fixing a quick meal, the young men almost instantly fell asleep, they were so exhausted. They were awakened very early the next morning, with the news that the Lamanites were in hot pursuit. They ran from the large army again that day, and rested the second day. Again, they arose early on the third day, and tried to keep ahead of the enemy.

Turkon realized that the Lamanites must be in excellent shape to keep up with the youthful warriors. The year's respite in Judea had hardened and strengthened his muscles, but they were still slowly catching up with him and the rest of Helaman's young army. During the third day's march, the spies told Helaman that the Lamanite army had stopped.

Helaman gathered his young warriors together, and stood on a large rock where they could all see and hear him. "My noble sons, I salute you for your perseverance thus far. We're now faced with a dilemma. The largest Lamanite army has discontinued chasing us. It could be that they are setting a trap for us, thinking we will surmise that Antipus' army has caught up with them. Instead, they will wait to annihilate us from off the face of the earth.

Or it could be true that Antipus has caught them from behind, in which case they could be fighting a savage battle at this very time. What say ye, my brethren?" Nevertheless that they had never fought before, they unanimously showed great courage in explaining in unison, "Let us go forth, in the integrity of youth, and we do not believe God will forsake us." Wow. Helaman had never seen such bravery in any of his troops before, and he was mightily impressed with his "sons."

Helaman turned his young army around, and hurriedly led his army back to where the Lamanites had stopped. What they found was a huge slaughter on both sides. In fact, because they were so outnumbered, many of Antipus' men had given up, and were running for their lives, especially when they saw their leader fall. Antipus, was killed after valiantly killing many Lamanites, but behold, he became worn out and felt the sword which found his neck.. But when the remaining Nephite army saw Helaman's force attacking the rear of the Lamanites, they grew hopeful and turned around to fight again.

The Lamanites were now surrounded, and they began to be faint of heart. In fact, they were being hewn down in frightful speed. Helaman watched his young soldiers fight so courageously, and with the "strength of God" within them, that he was sorely amazed. The battle lasted another couple of hours, with the Nephites and their armor gaining ground. Thousands and thousands gave up their weapons, and became prisoners of war.

Helaman searched the battle field for any of his dead warriors, and was shocked to not being able to find one of them. They all had serious wounds, and some had passed out because of loss of blood, but every one of them had survived! He later reported, "Behold, to my great joy, there had not one soul of them fallen to the earth; yea, they seemed to fight with the strength of God, insomuch that when these Lamanites saw these, my sons, fight so valiantly, they gave up and became our prisoners."

During the battle, Turkon's arm became very heavy and painful from holding it up and swinging it so much, but whenever that happened, he felt a surge of power envelope him. He knew this power wasn't his own, but a heavenly gift bestowed upon him and his fellow warriors as a result of their great faith.

And with almost his entire body saturated with blood, some of his own, and most from the enemy, (not to mention sometimes wiping the gooey liquid from his eyes), he hardly felt a sword pierce through his left shoulder, slicing muscle, tissue, and sinew; due to his adrenaline rush. Nor the cut to his left arm which travelled to the bone. But now that the battle was over, the pain began setting in, making it almost unbearable. But he kept the pain to himself, as did his friends and compatriots.

CHAPTER 4

THE AFTERMATH

Turkon went to a small creek nearby, where clear, clean water bubbled over the jagged rocks, and he cleaned himself off, while his friend, Jacob, helped him dress the wounds, and make a sling for his left arm. He then cleaned and dressed Jacob's wounds. He had an ugly gash on his head, which matted his head with the tar-like clotted blood. He also had many superficial skin wounds which needed attention.

Illustrated by Sterling Day

Turkon resting near creek

Thankfully, there was a reprieve from fighting for a few months to enable the men to recover from their injuries. The final tally:

9,000 prisoners of war

13,000 enemy casualties

4,500 Nephite casualties

Unbeknown to his men, Helaman slipped away to find a secluded spot to pray. "Oh, how great and holy art thou,God! I am cognizant of thy Omnipotence and thy great power. From the east to the west, from the north to the south, never has there been such faith and reward among all human battles. How I wish to mightily thank thee with every inch of my being. To deliver my stripling young warriors in such an awesome way, I can never repay thee. But I do wish to thank-thee with all my heart. May I here-to-for never let thee down, in thy Son's Holy Name, Amen.

Heleman praying

When Ammoron, the king of the Lamanites, heard of the rout his men experienced, and the number of prisoners Helaman took, he was angry and disheartened. He wrote an epistle to Helaman, offering to give back the city of Antiparah if he would give the king the many prisoners he captured. "Not a chance," replied Helaman. He knew that Antiparah was not heavily guarded, and he could win the city back easily with his new army. So Helaman sent an epistle back to Ammoron, stating he would exchange prisoners, but Ammoron refused.

CHAPTER 5

THE BATTLE OF CUMENI

When the Lamanites in the city of Antiparah realized the new found strength of the Nephite army, they deserted the city at night and fled to the more fortified cities. So the Nephites were able to receive that city without one soul being lost! And so ended the 28th year of the reign of the judges.

In the commencement of the 29th year, Helaman received 60 more warriors from the People of Ammon, and 6,000 more Nephite troops from Zarahemla, as well as many more provisions. With such a strong force, Helaman reasoned that this was a good time to attack the Lamanites in the fortified city of Cumeni. The Nephite army surrounded the city and kept them from receiving any supplies.

At night, they pitched their tents and slept on their swords, in case the Lamanite snuck out of the city when darkness set in. Just as they suspected, the Lamanites did try this numerous times, but each time their blood was spilt, not the Nephites. Sure enough, a vast column containing many provisions tried to enter the city at night. Instead, they were interrupted, and the supplies were sent to the city of Judea. They also sent their prisoners to Zarahemla, where they could be contained more easily.

At first, the Lamanites stubbornly stayed within the city, but they began to lose all hope of succor after many days without food and supplies. It wasn't long before they surrendered. The Nephites had to watch many thousands of these new prisoners, and it took all their time to watch over them. In fact, they would break out of these enclosures constantly, and fight with stones and sticks or whatever else they could find. Already, the Nephites had slain more than 2,000 of them in this manner.

Helaman decided to march these new prisoners to Zarhemla, as there was barely enough food for his men, let alone the prisoners of war. Helaman ordered Gid to take part of the army and march the prisoners to Zarahemla. Meanwhile, he ordered the rest of his army to stay in Cumeni. However, the very next day, a large contingent of Lamanites attacked Cumeni. Again, another ferocious battle was underway.

The 2,060 young warriors were again fighting like lions among sheep, with the enemy falling left and right. In fact, Helaman reported that these stripling young warriors obeyed every order with strictness. Turkon must have killed seven or eight them before he was struck down. He was pierced on his right side by a sword, as two Lamanite soldiers were attacking him at the same time. A large, powerful Lamanite was swinging his sword directly at him, while another snuck up behind him and stabbed him in his side. The wound bled out, and he fainted on the spot. The Lamanites thought he was dead, so they moved forward.

As the battle raged on, it was pretty obvious to everyone that the Lamanites were slowly gaining ground. Then another miracle happened. Gid suddenly appeared with his army and fell upon the Lamanites with such ferocity that the Lamanites panicked and began to run. They retreated to the city of Manti.

Helaman ordered his men to dig deep pits to bury the dead on both sides. If these bodies were allowed to lay in the hot sun, the stench would have been horrendous. Not to mention the maggots and flies they would produce. As men scoured the battle site, they found 200 of the stripling young warriors, including Turkon, unconscious but still breathing. Any wounded Lamanites were killed immediately, as rations were low.

Turkon's wound was sterilized with a hot poker, and wrapped in a clean dressing to prevent any ubiquitous infection from entering the deep cut. The wound was so deep it would take many weeks, if not months, to totally heal. Again, the Nephite soldiers were in awe of these stripling young soldiers, as it was so uncanny that not even one of them ever died, though they all suffered many wounds. They knew this was not normal, and that an unseen hand was at work with these amazing young men.

After the dust had settled, Helaman approached Gid to find out what happened. Gid explained that there were so many Lamanite prisoners, they kept trying to escape. They would run out of formation, pick up rocks, sticks, or whatever they could find and try to battle their captors. Gid had 5,000 men to guard the 13,000 prisoners, and it was a constant struggle to keep them in line.

To add to the bedlam, Nephite spies came running into camp one night and declared there was another huge Lamanite army on their way to Cumeni. The prisoners heard this, and gathered strength from this declaration. They rose up, on mass, and rebelled against their guards. They were literally running themselves onto the Nephite swords. Many of them met their death in this way, while the remainder fled to their freedom. At first, the Nephites chased them, but gave up as the Lamanites were too fast for them to catch.

Instead, they hurried back to Cumeni, just in time to enter the raging battle before them, and turn the tide of battle towards the Nephites. It was good that the Nephites had routed their enemies. Now Turkon and the other troops could concentrate on healing their wounds, both psychcologically, emotionally, and physically. The pain Turkon experienced was unreal, and there were no medications to lighten it. The War is a nasty business, and it can destroy a person in more ways than one. Turkon and the other stripling young warriors were thankful for the rest. They needed to keep the faith, and pray continually, if they expected the Master's continual concern and protection they desperately needed.

Not only did they rehabilitate their wounds, but they continued with their exercises, always trying to keep and even ameliorating their fighting skills. You never knew when the Lamanites would strike again. In a way, that was the worst torture of all, the suspense of when they would be attacked again.

Helaman in his office

CHAPTER 6

THE CAPTURE OF MANTI

Now the Nephite army wished to attack the city of Manti, where the Lamanites were holed up, but they were wary of any traps, like the one they were suckered into at Judea, so they stayed inside the fortified walls, and refused to come out and fight. They also remembered how they were defeated last time, in spite of the fact they vastly outnumbered the Nephites, they had another incentive of hiding behind the walls of Manti.

Because of the last few battles, even though they had won, the Nephite army had measurably dwindled until they became a tiny shell of what they used to be. How they were going to conquest Manti became a huge concern. Helaman decided to wait in Cumeni until reinforcements again arrived from Zarahemla, along with needed provisions.

The only problem with this strategy was that the Lamanites were also receiving reinforcements and provisions on a daily basis. The Lamanites did make a few excursions at night to make sure the Nephites would not receive any more provisions, and it kept the Nephites in limbo for many months. It wasn't long before the Nephite army was about to perish for want of food.

Before all was lost, a contingent of 2,000 soldiers arrived from Zarahemla, along with many provisions, to stave off starvation. Meanwhile, spies notified Helaman that the Lamanites seemed more innumerable than they had ever been before, and reinforcements kept on coming weekly. Helaman found out much later the reason Zarahemla wasn't sending him more men and provisions was that Zarahemla was involved in a civil war involving the king-men, or those who wanted a king, against Pahoran and the democratic government. But that's another story.

Meanwhile, Helaman and his men prayed mightily to God every day, wondering what they should do. Peace came within their hearts that the Lord was watching over them, and that He would eventually deliver them. After all, didn't He rescue the Israelites against the pharaoh's chariots by drowning them in the Red Sea? If God could save the children of Israel, then why not them?

They girded up their strength and determined to go forth against the Lamanites, as they were fighting for their way of life, liberty, their wives and children, their lands and possessions. After a long march, they arrived near the city of Manti, and pitched their tents in the wilderness. By this time, it was the 30th year of the reign of the judges, and four years since Helaman recruited him in the lands of Ammon. In fact, Turkon was now 21 years old, and sporting a well-kept beard.

The next morning, they saw the Nephite army on the borders of the wilderness. They sent out spies to see how large their army was. To their delight, they came back with the news that the Nephites were a small shadow from what they once were. Compared with the numerous hosts of the Lamanites, the Nephites didn't have a chance. When Helaman realized that the

Lamanites were preparing for war, he decided to send Gid with a small number of men, and Teomner with another small group, to hide in the wilderness.

Now Gid was on the right and Teomner on the left. Conversely, the rest of the army stayed with me where we originally pitched our tents. And behold, the Lamanites did come forth with their numerous hosts, itching for a battle. When Helaman saw this, he had his army run away from them into the wilderness.

Upon seeing the Nephite running for their lives, they ran faster to catch them and destroy them from off the face of the earth. But as soon as Helaman's army passed by Gid and Teomner, they came out of their hiding places and killed the straggling Lamanite spies that were tagging behind the huge Lamanite army.

Then they hustled over to Manti, and to their utter joy, found it was only being guarded by a few guards. They easily slew the guards and inhabited the huge fortifications of the city. Meanwhile, Helaman's force was able to outrun the large contingent of Lamanite warriors, and they took their course towards the large capital city of Zarahemla.

Now when the Lamanites saw they were headed towards Zarahemla, they became afraid, as they knew how powerful the Nephite armies were in said city. Or they thought that Helaman could be leading them into another trap. Either way, it was not good.

By this time, it was beginning to be night, so the Lamanites pitched their tents in the wilderness, supposing the Nephites were still marching towards Zarahemla. Rather than allowing his weary men to sleep, he ordered his men to march around the

Lamanite encampment while they slept, and reach Manti before the Lamanites awoke the next morning! So by this strategy, Helaman was able to obtain the mighty city of Manti without the shedding of blood.

When the Lamanites saw what had happened, fear struck their hearts, and they fled with the many Nephite women and children that they had abducted while inhabiting the three Nephite cities before they were defeated.

Victory

CHAPTER 7

THE HOMECOMING

Helaman, and his army, which included the sons of Ammon, remained in the city of Manti for many months until General Moroni led a great army and vanquished the king-men who had usurped the government and brought great anguish throughout the land. When peace again ruled the lands, Helaman returned to the ministry, and the soldiers returned home.

The stripling young warriors formed themselves into the two battalions that Helaman had earlier organized, and marched the six days to be back home. Turkon was so excited, he could hardly contain himself. He wanted to run ahead of the battalion and be with his family before the others, but he knew he must use patience and control his passions. Besides, he was still the leader of his group of 100; and to think that not one was lost. How could any of them deny the existence of God and all of His tender mercies towards the stripling young men?

After what seemed like an eternity, the young warriors finally reached their homes and celebrated their safe arrival. The excitement in these communities was palpable. Everyone seemed to line the streets and watch the gallant young warriors march on by. Much applause and cheers could be heard throughout the land. "Our sons have returned to us," shouted one venerable old man, "Hallelujah and pass the bisquits," a euphemism he liked to say that made no sense.

Turkon's mother was the first to see her son in the family. She hugged and kissed Turkon til it became somewhat embarrassing. But Turkon didn't mind. He wanted to jump up and down himself. Then his Dad put his arm around his shoulder in a tight squeeze, and welcomed his son home. Then his two little brothers wanted to give their big brother a hug, as well as his 16 year old sister.

Turkon could hardly believe the change of his siblings after a four year sabbatical. After all, when he left, his sister was 12 yrs. old, and now she was a young lady at 16.

And waiting patiently in line there was Richelle. She hardly recognized him with his dark beard, but through the scruff, she could see the old Turkon. "It's true. It's me," replied Turkon. "Oh Turkon, I can hardly believe you're standing in front of me." And with many tears flowing from both of them, they hugged and kissed each other excitedly as if they would never see each other again.

"Oh Turkon, will you marry me? I don't want to wait another minute, in case something else will take you away from me." After getting over the shock of what she was proposing, he began to think it might be a good idea after all. "Well, uhh uh uh, well I don't see why not?" And with that, Richelle jumped into his arms and allowed him to twirl her around before a final kiss was shared between the two.

"Well then, we're going to look forward to our first grandchild then," replied his father. And after this, his mother and father shared a passionate kiss between the two of them. As the old saying goes, *"Love conquers all."*

Printed in the United States
By Bookmasters